I HELP

JOE CEPEDA

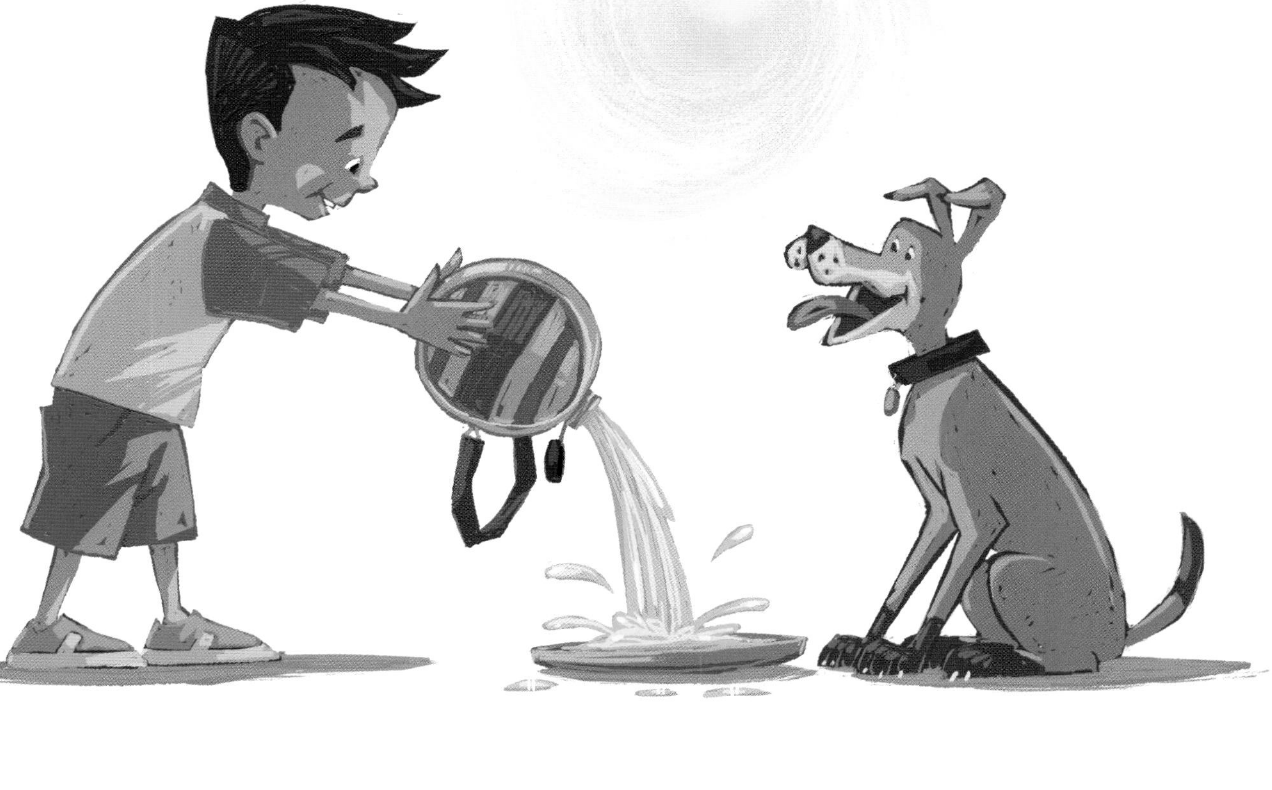

I Like to Read®

HOLIDAY HOUSE • NEW YORK

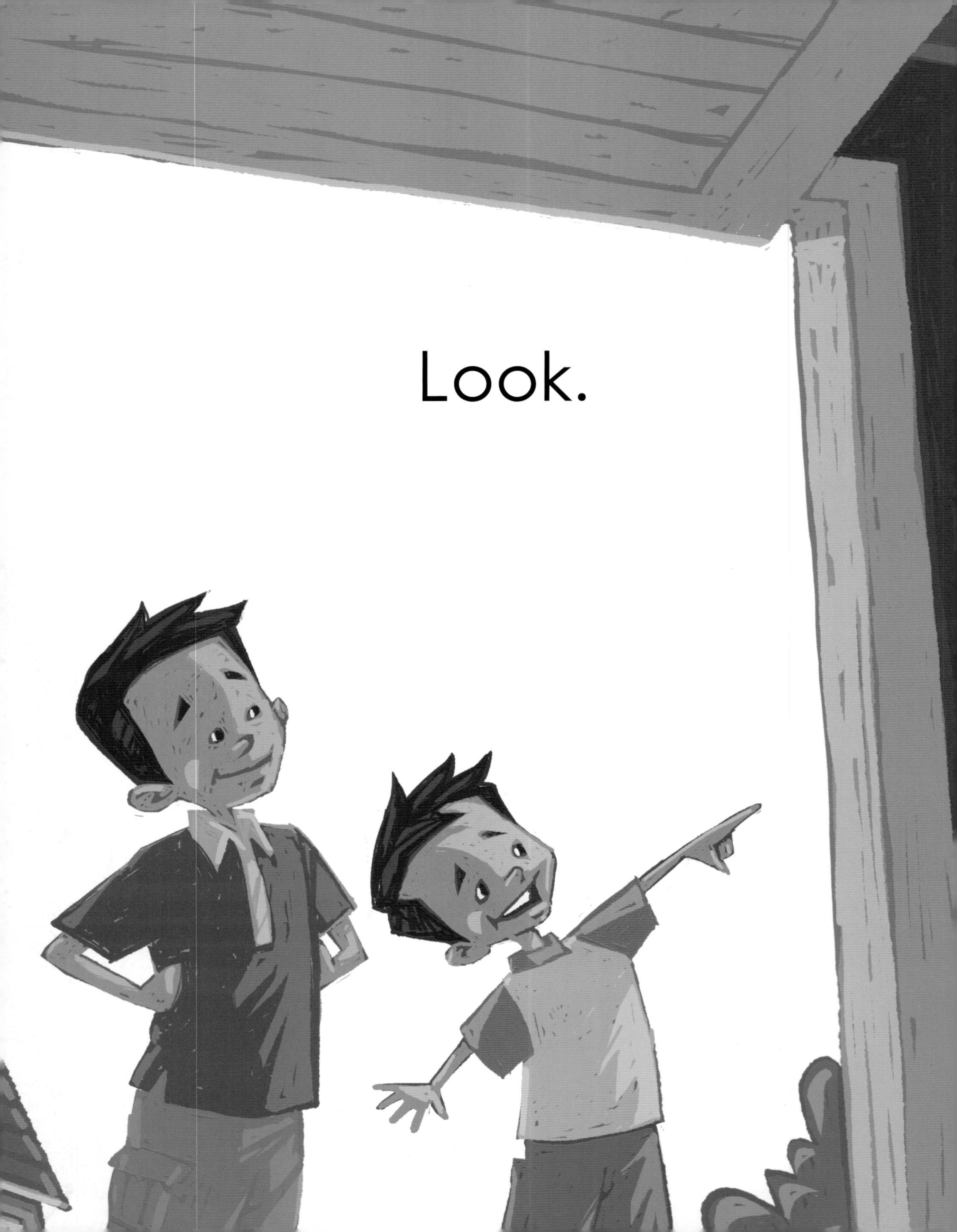
Look.

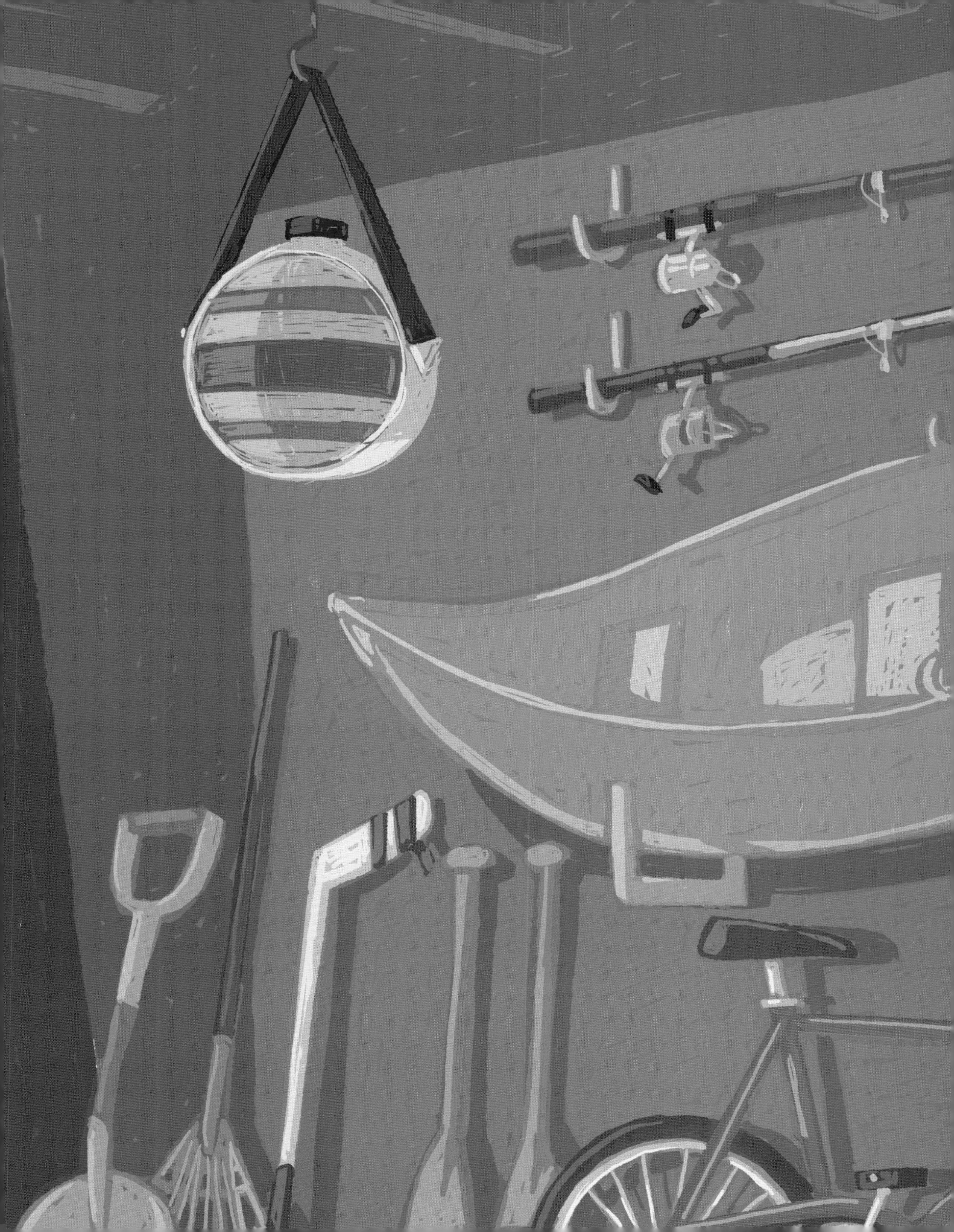

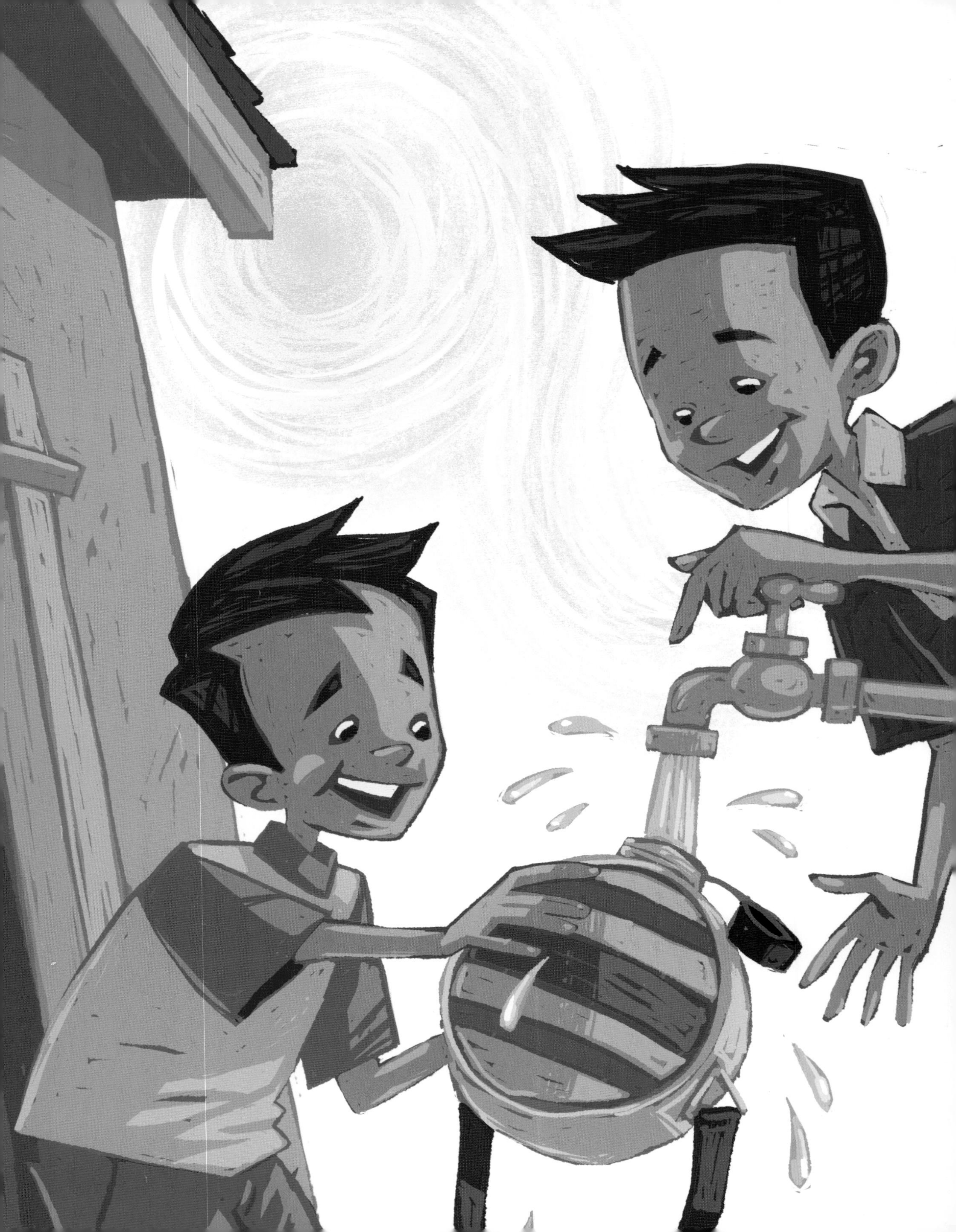

I go.

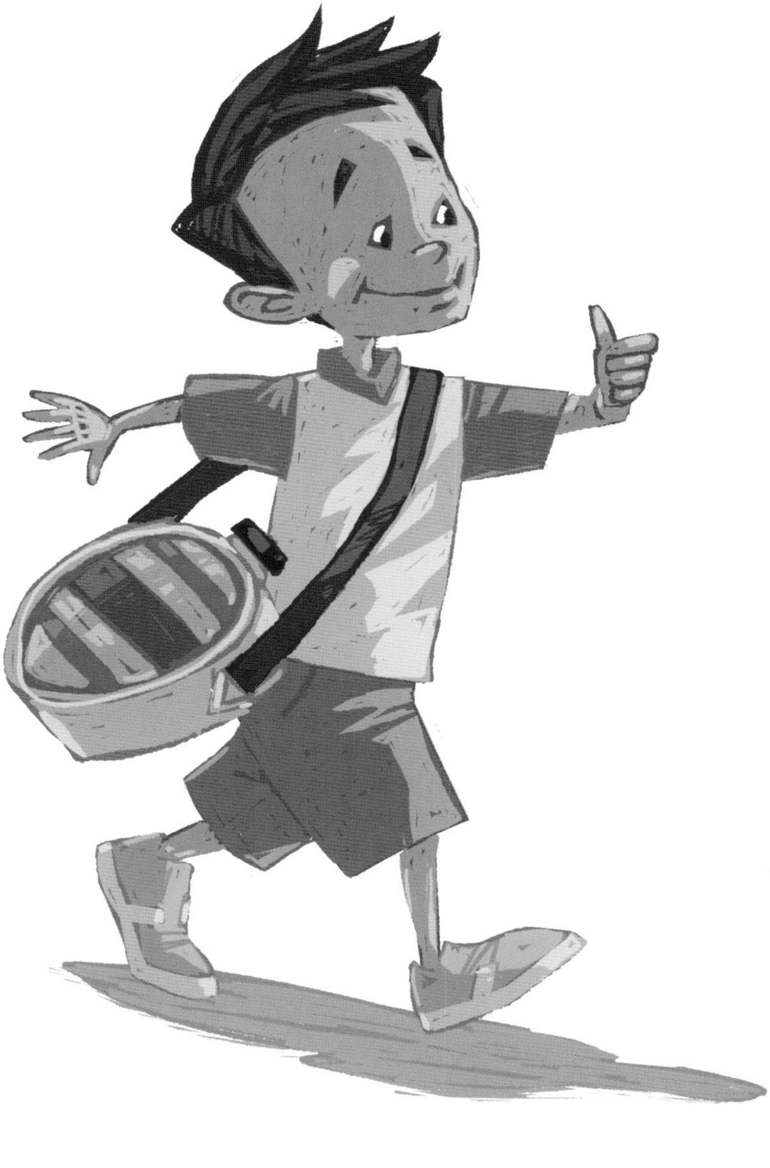

I see a dog.

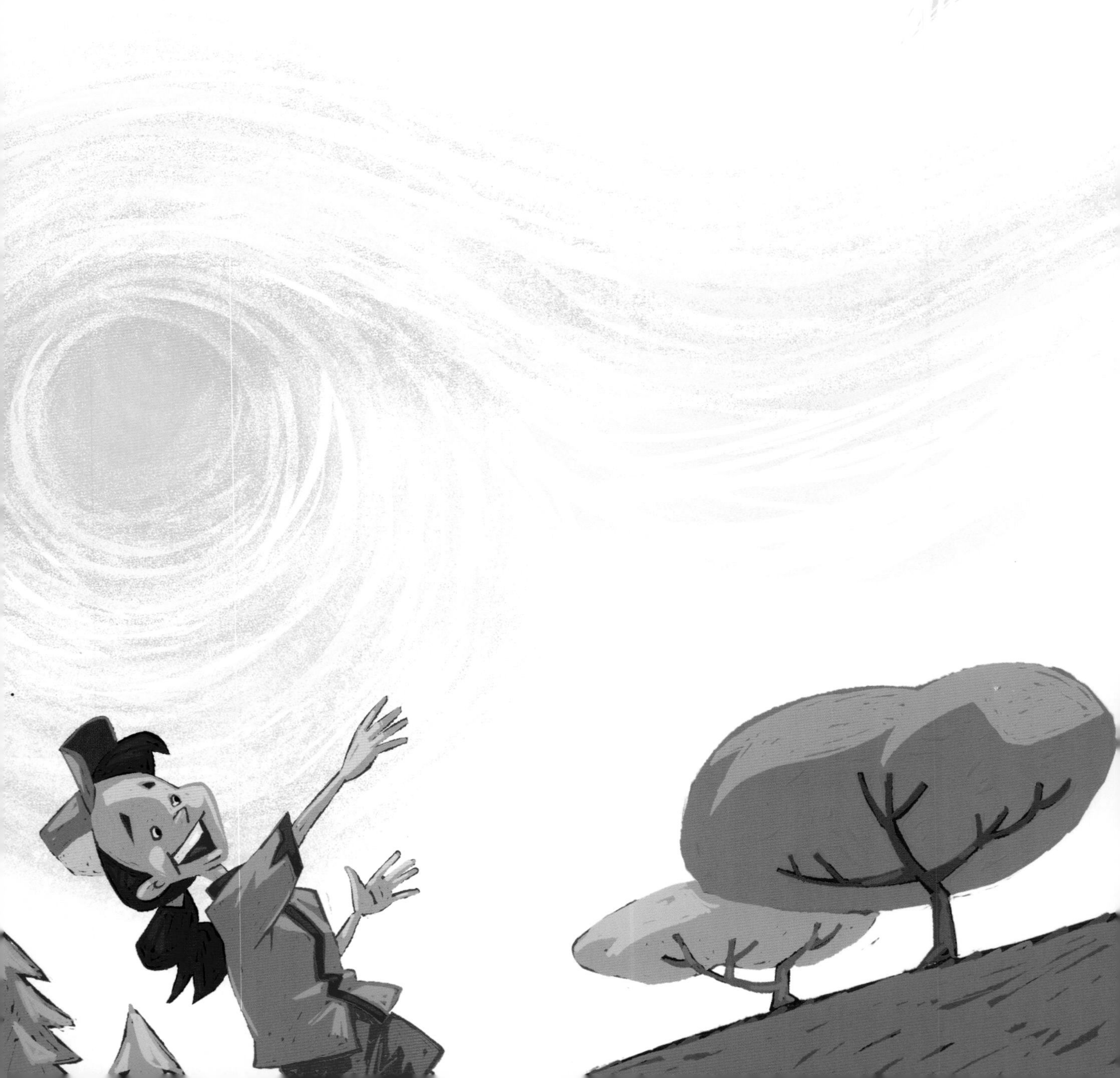

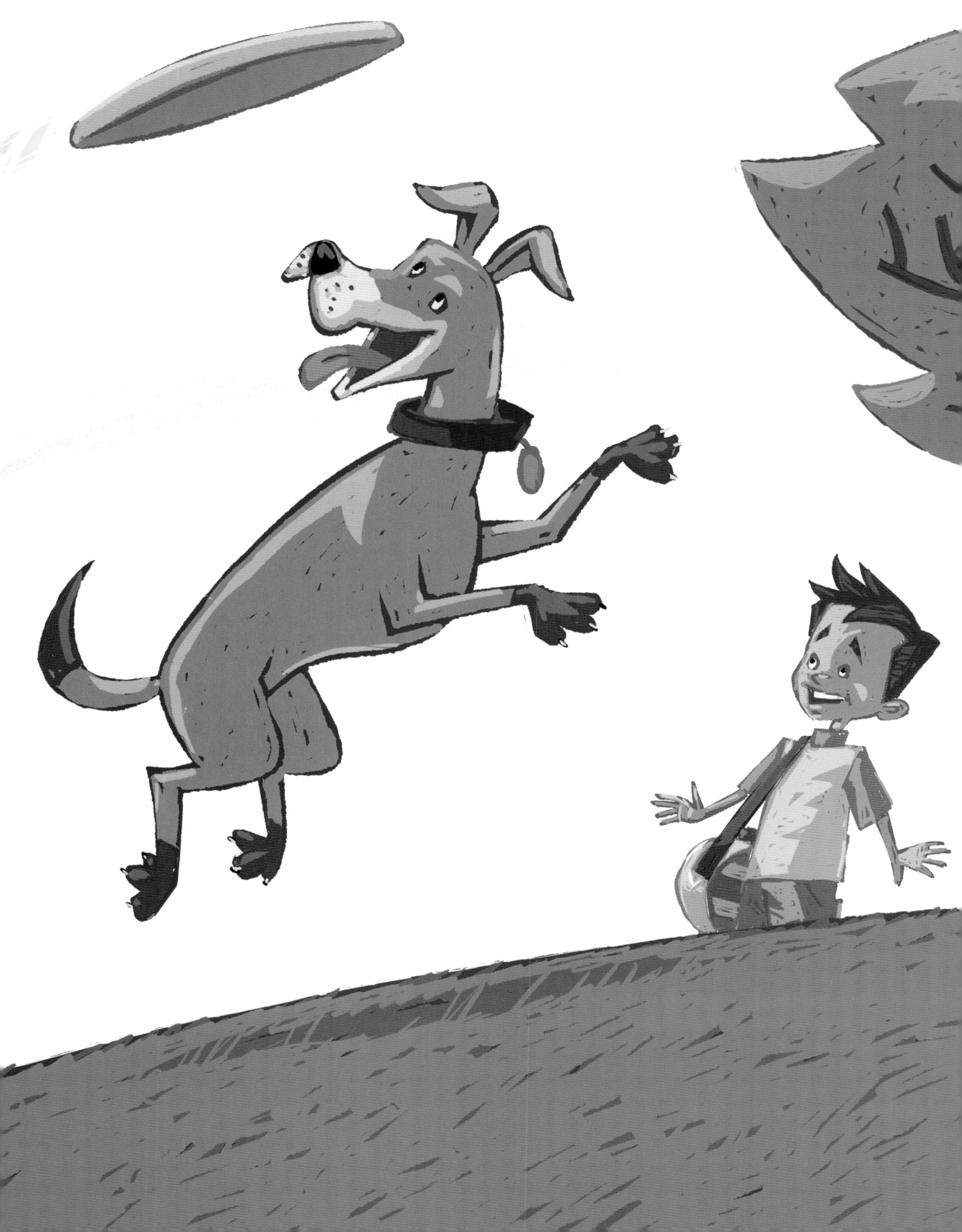

I help.

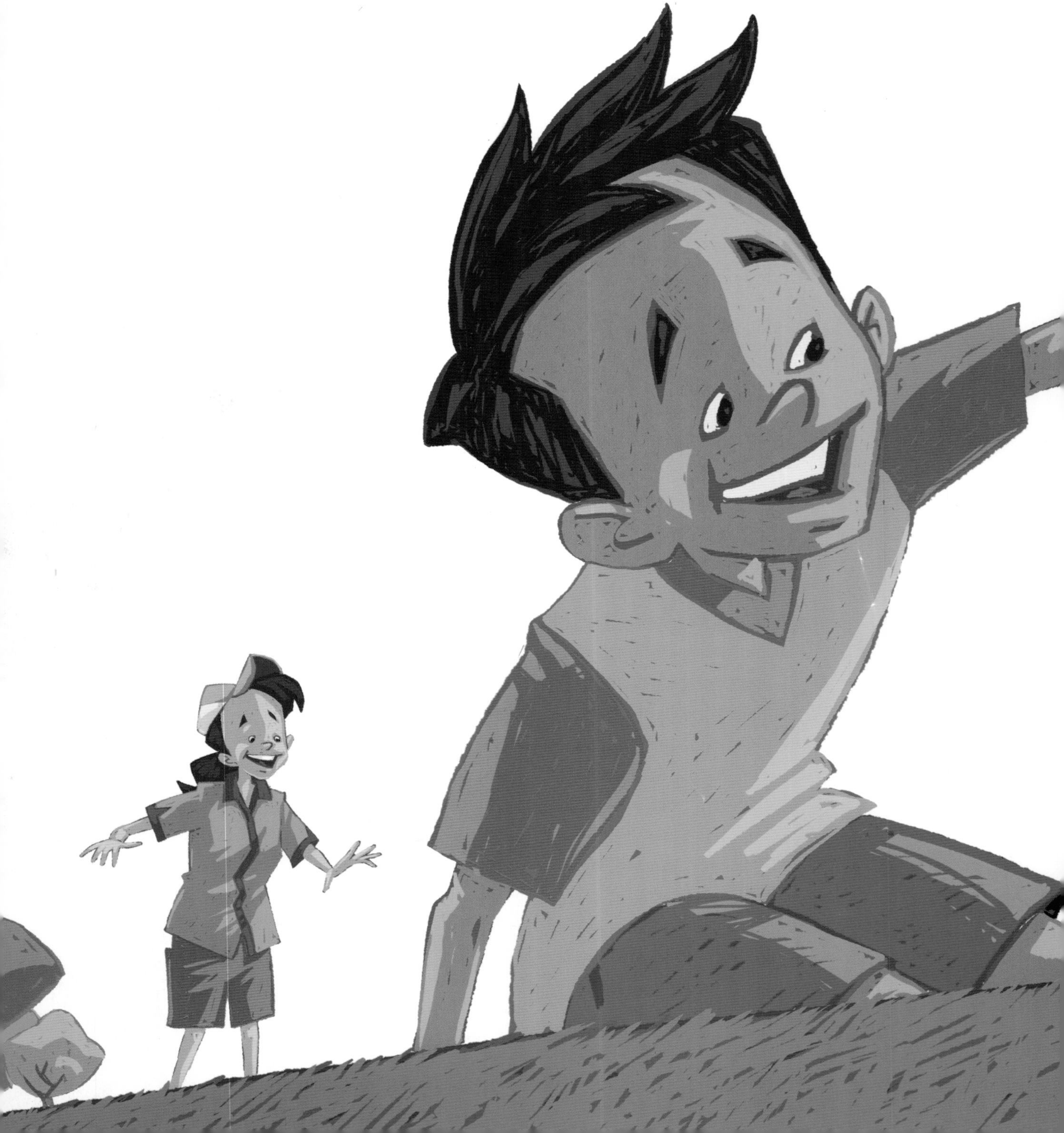

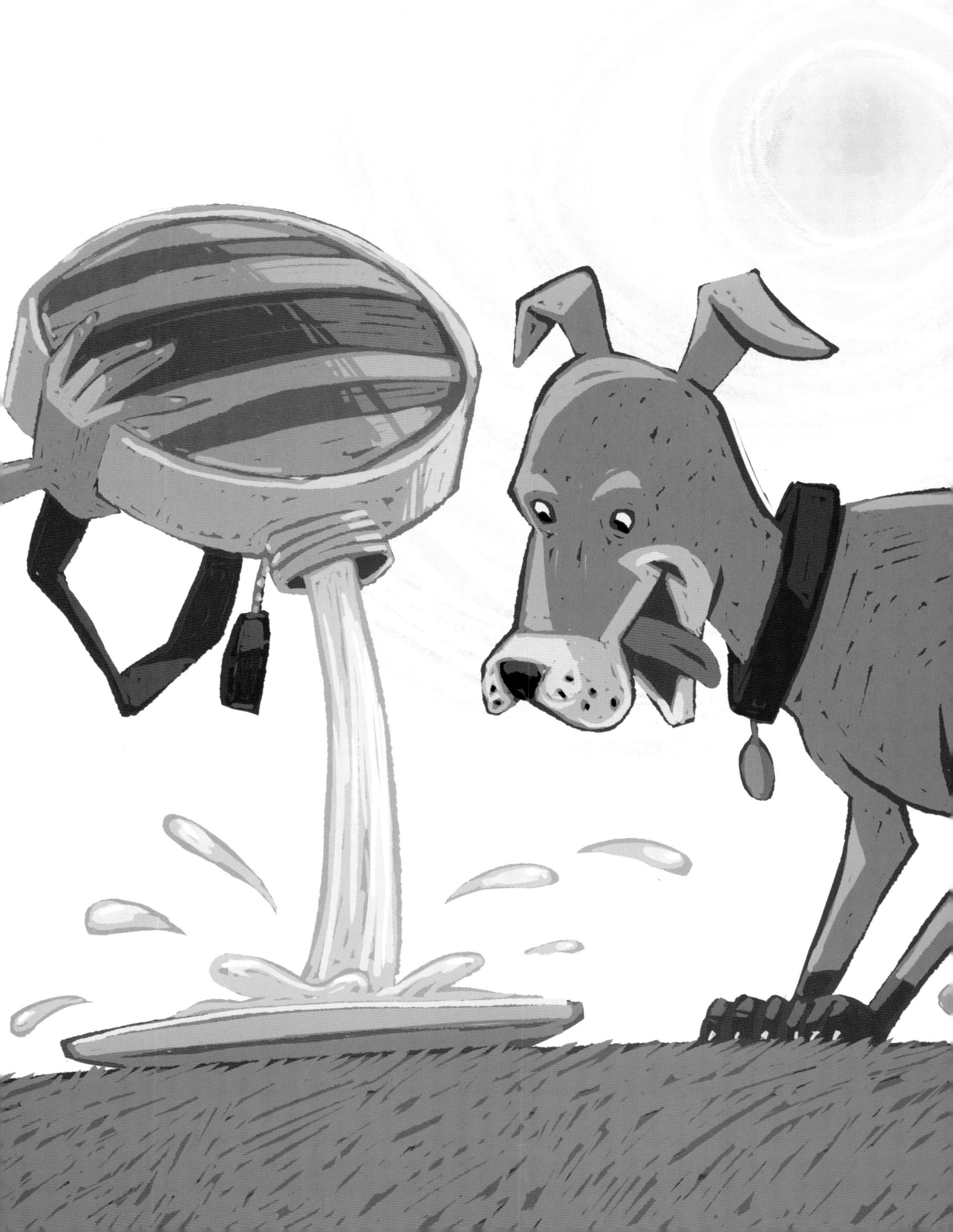

I help a man.

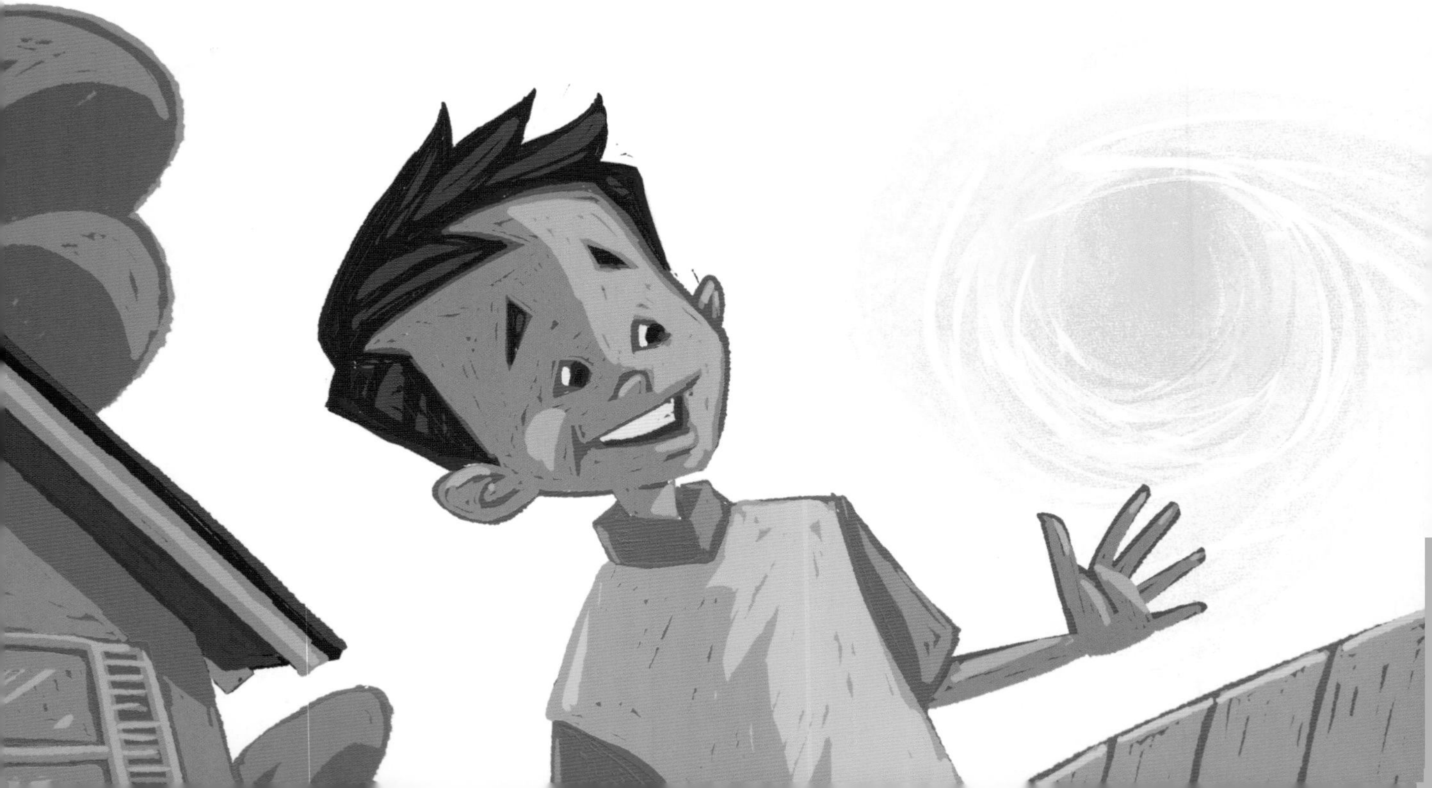

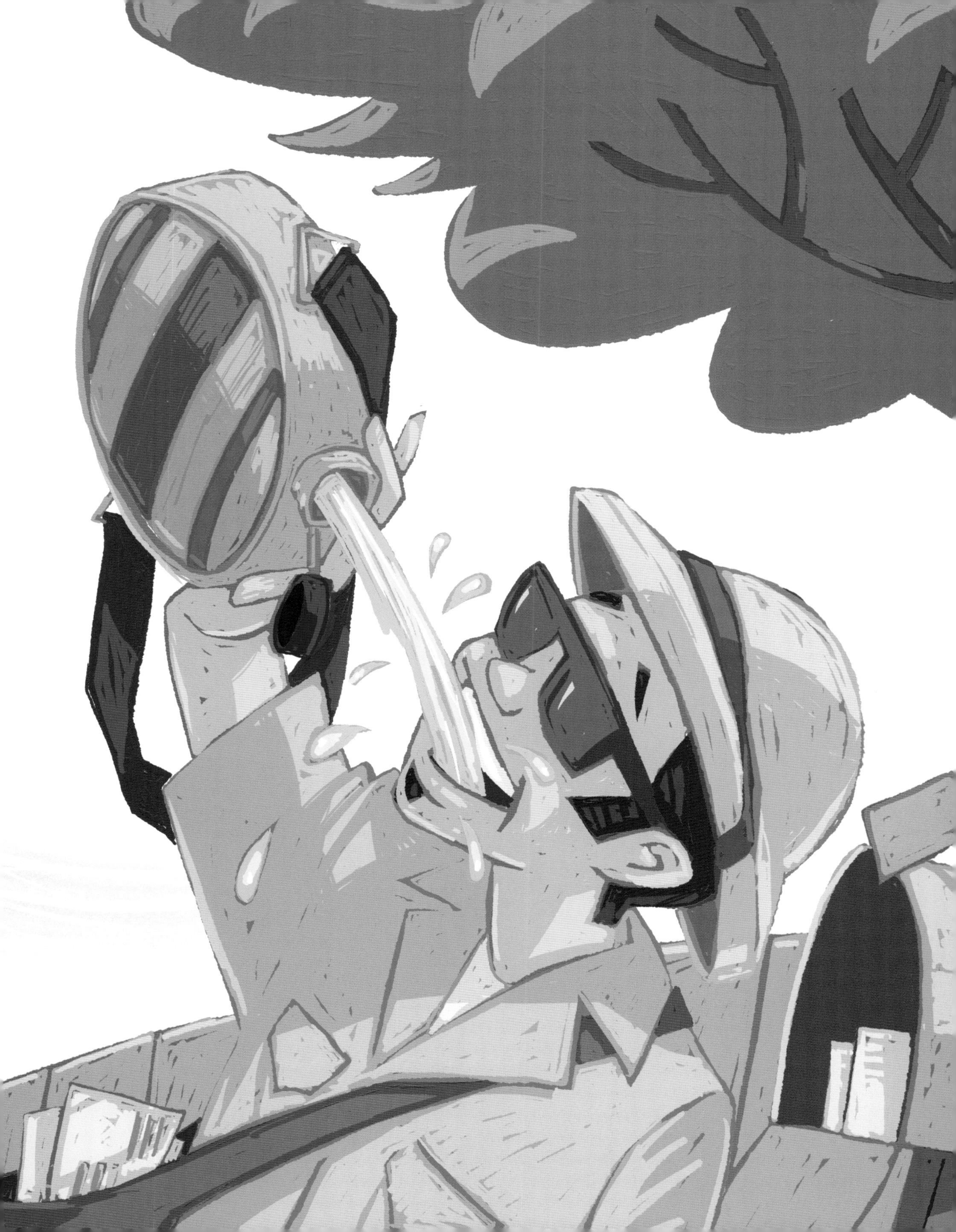

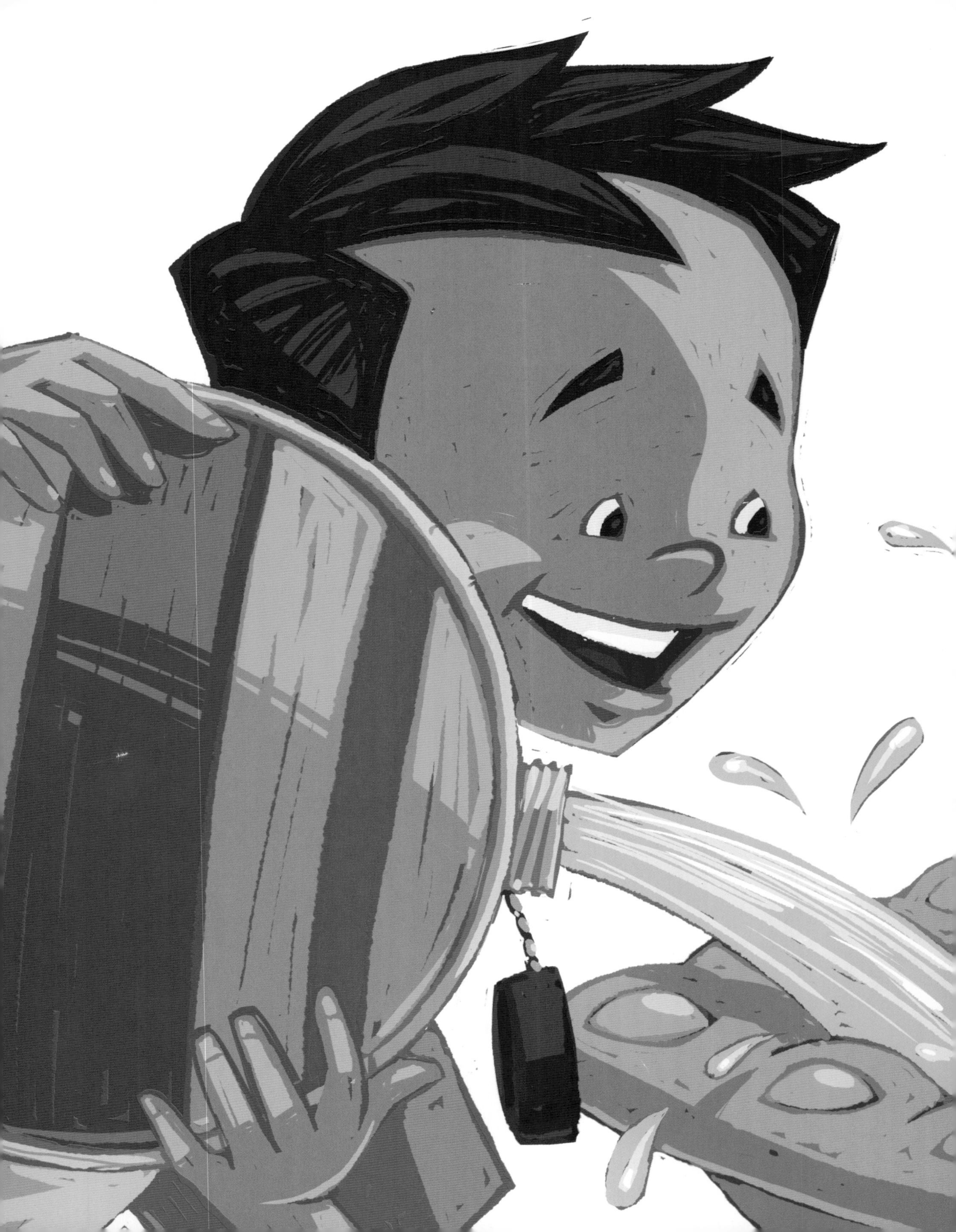

I help birds.

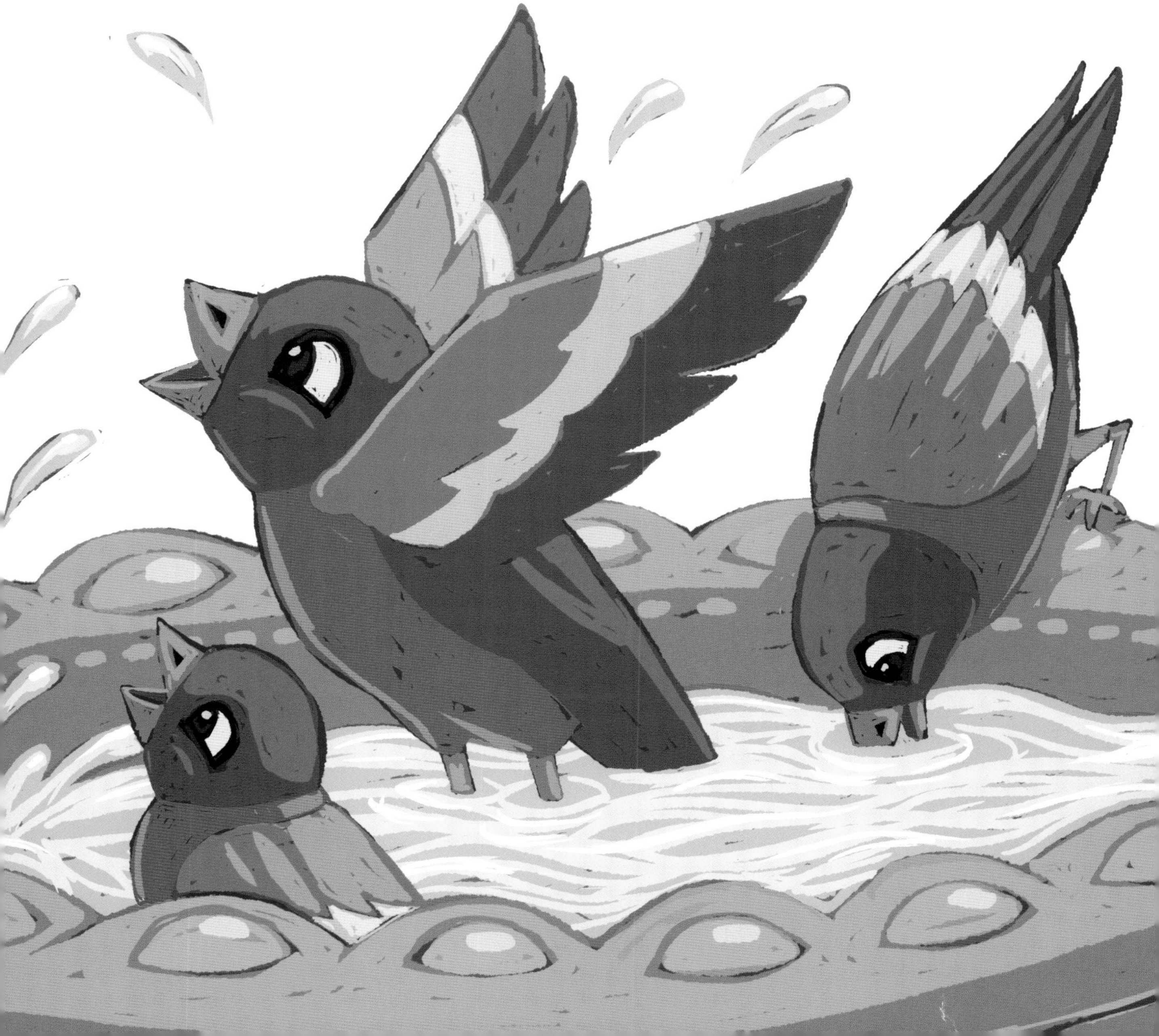

No water.

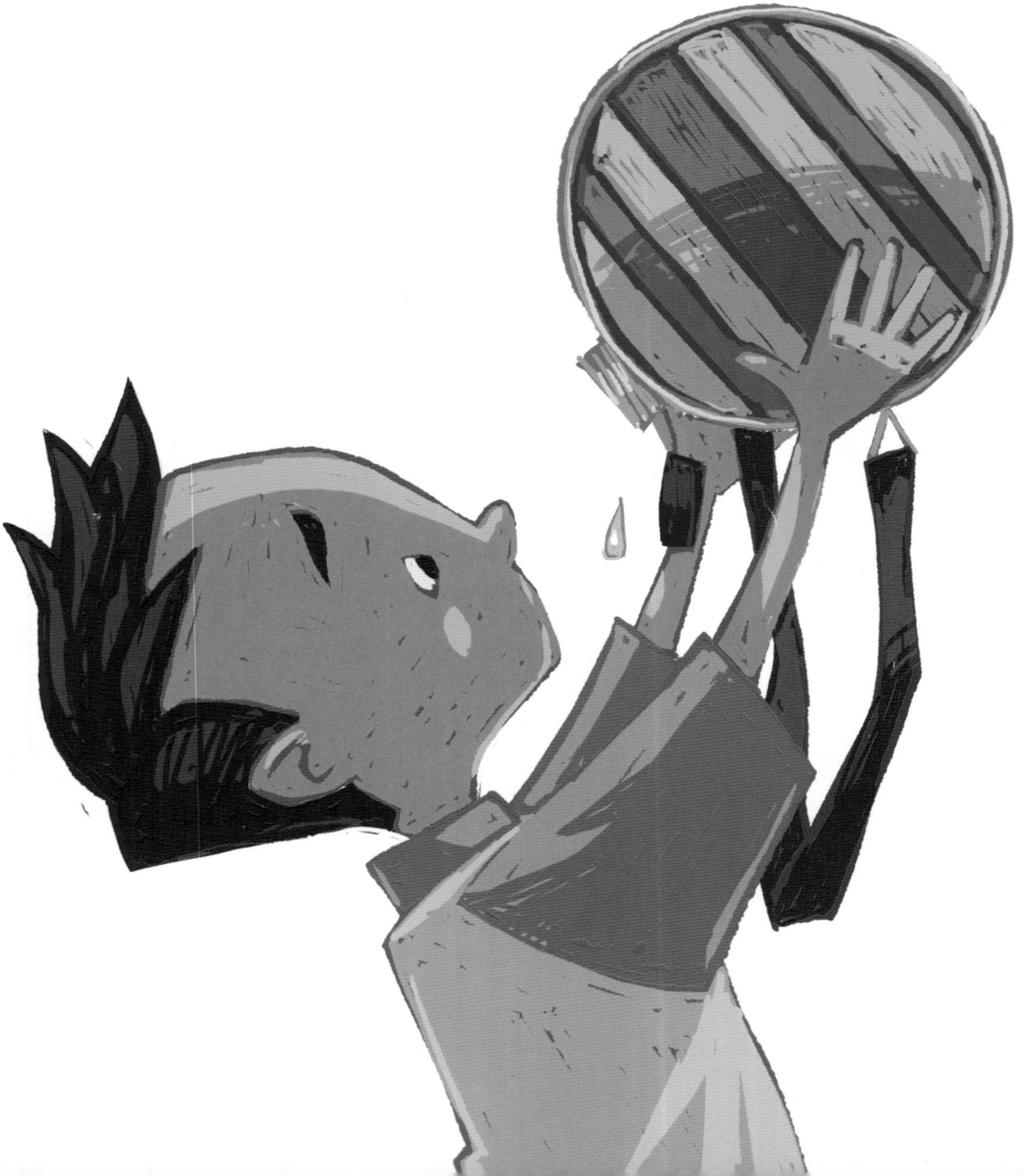

I go.

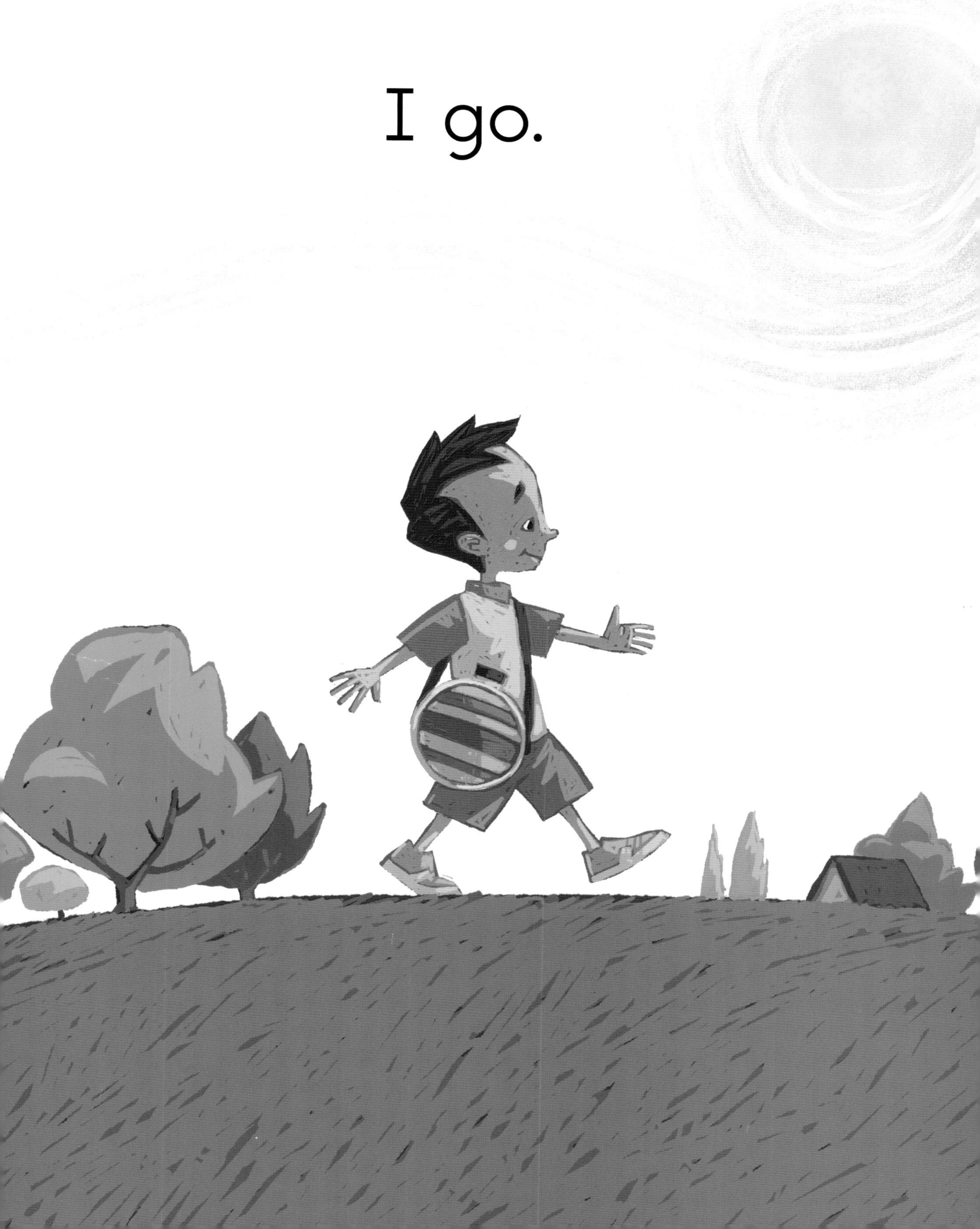

I see a band.

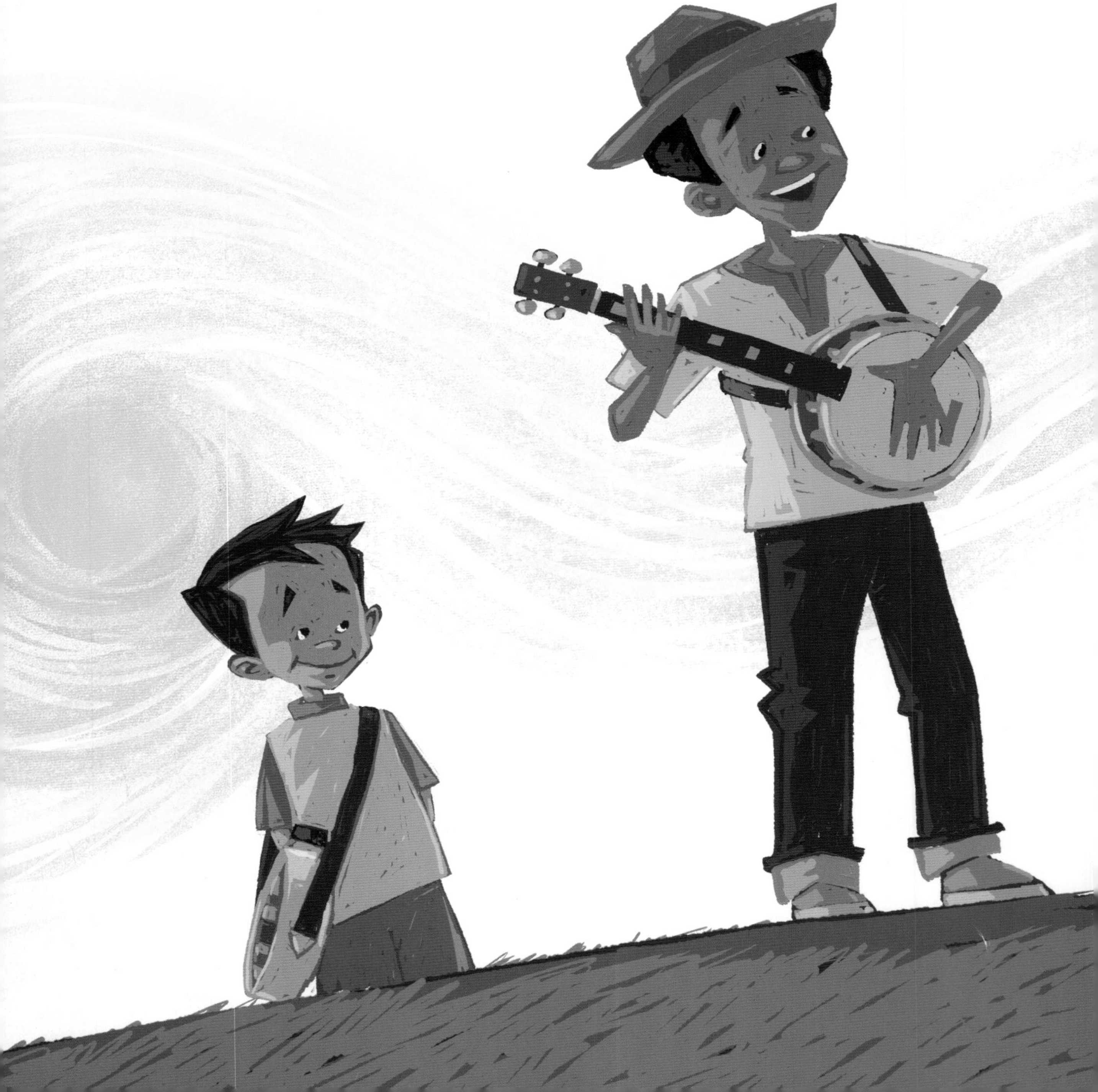

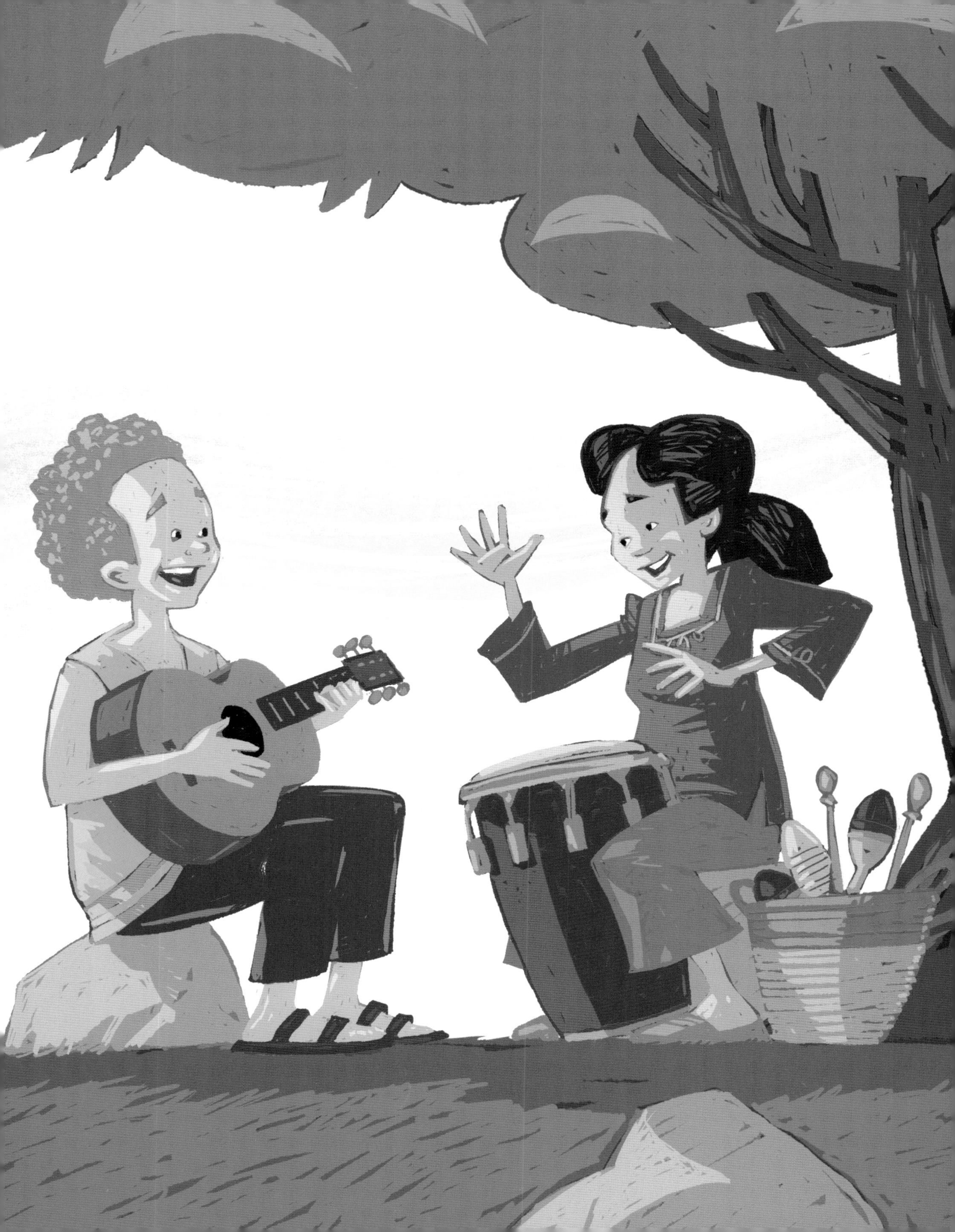

I help.

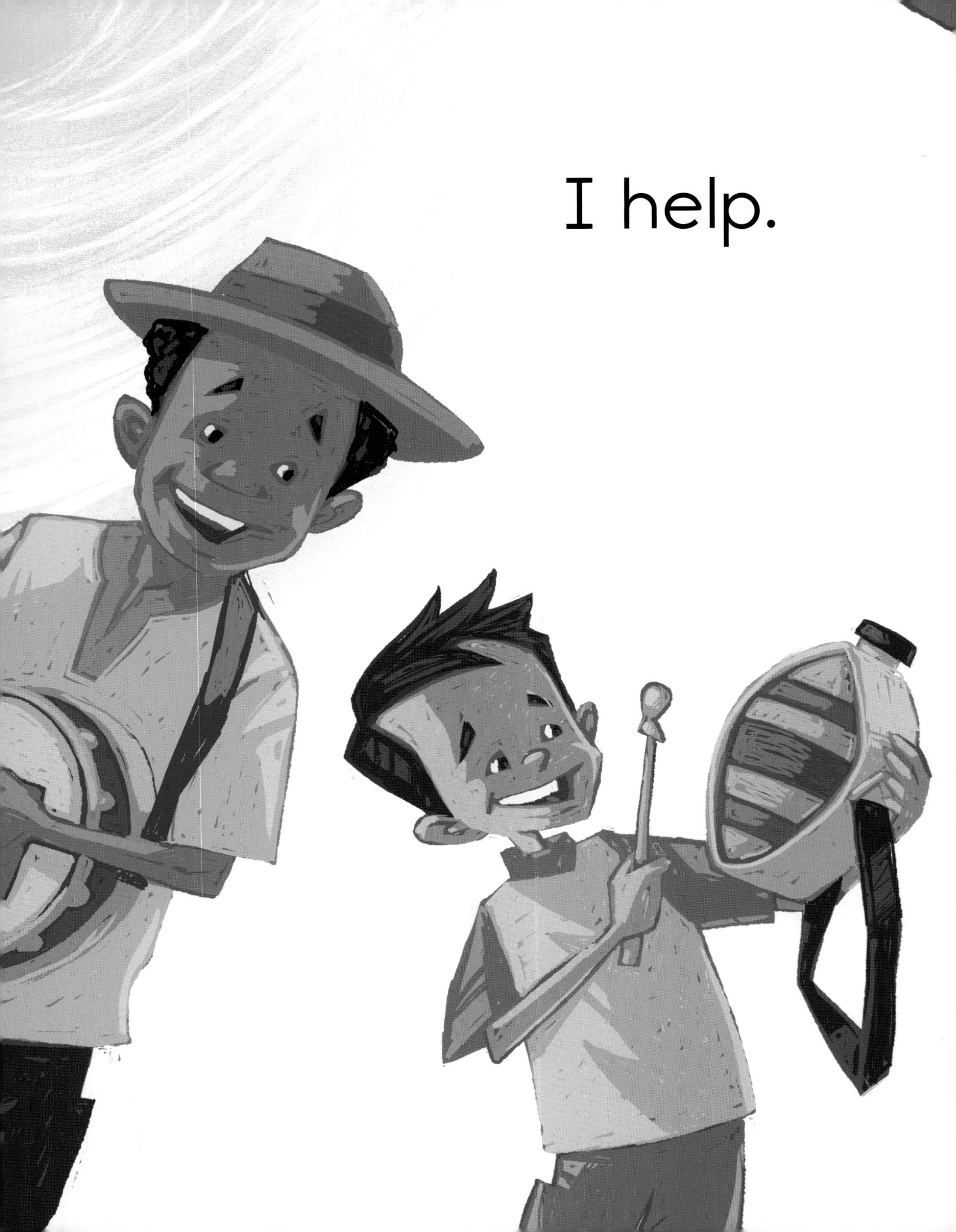

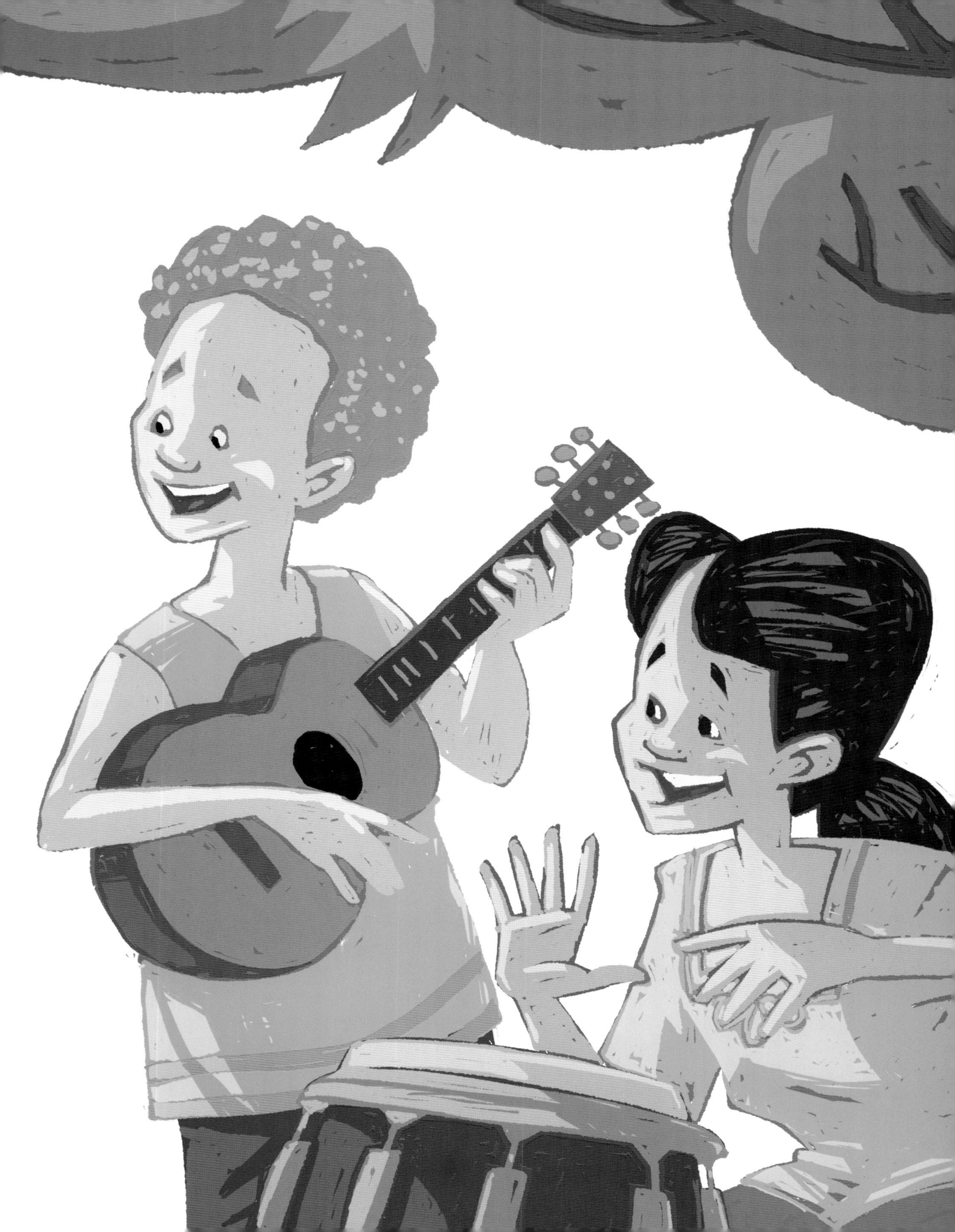

I see water.

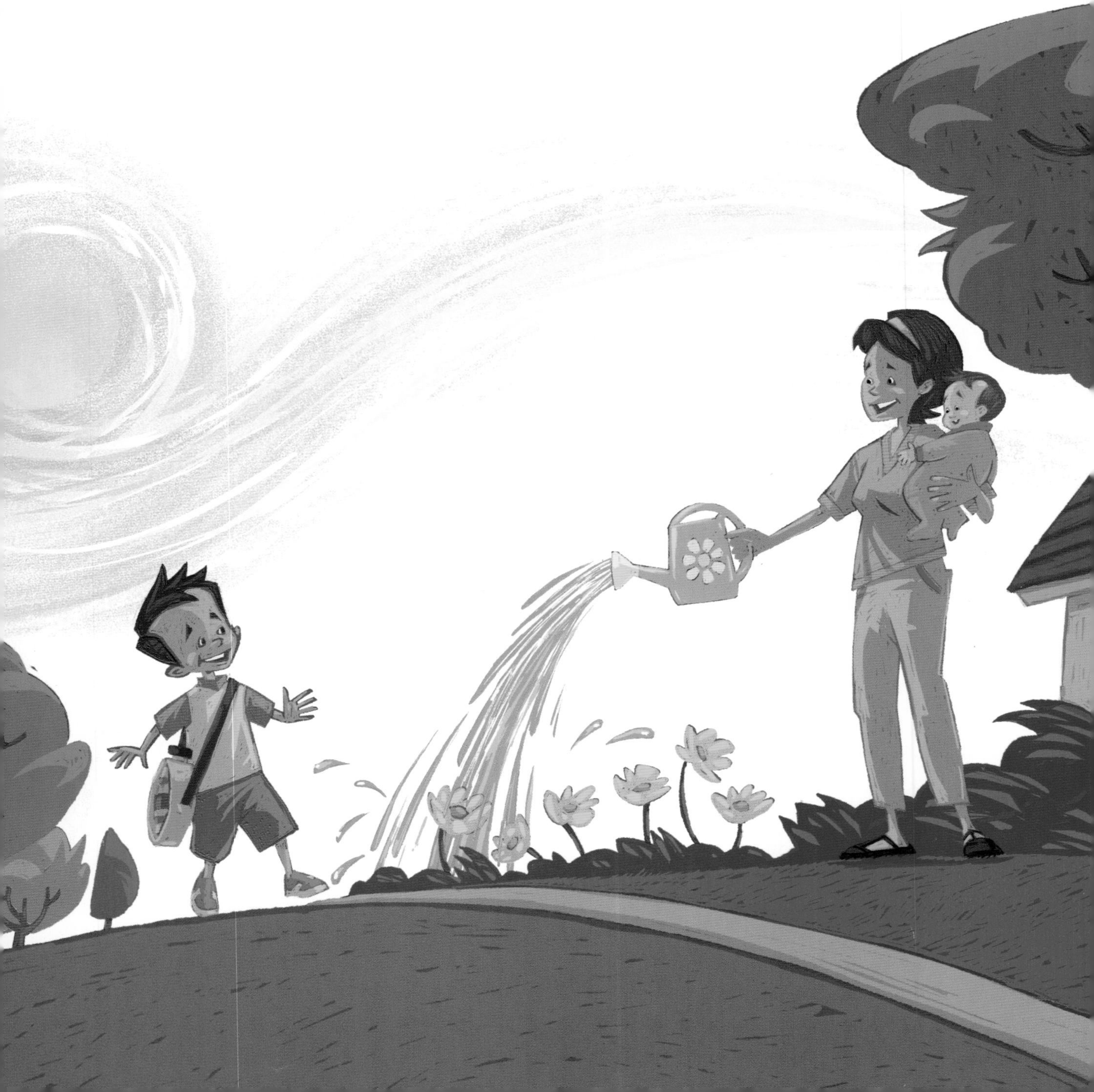

They help.

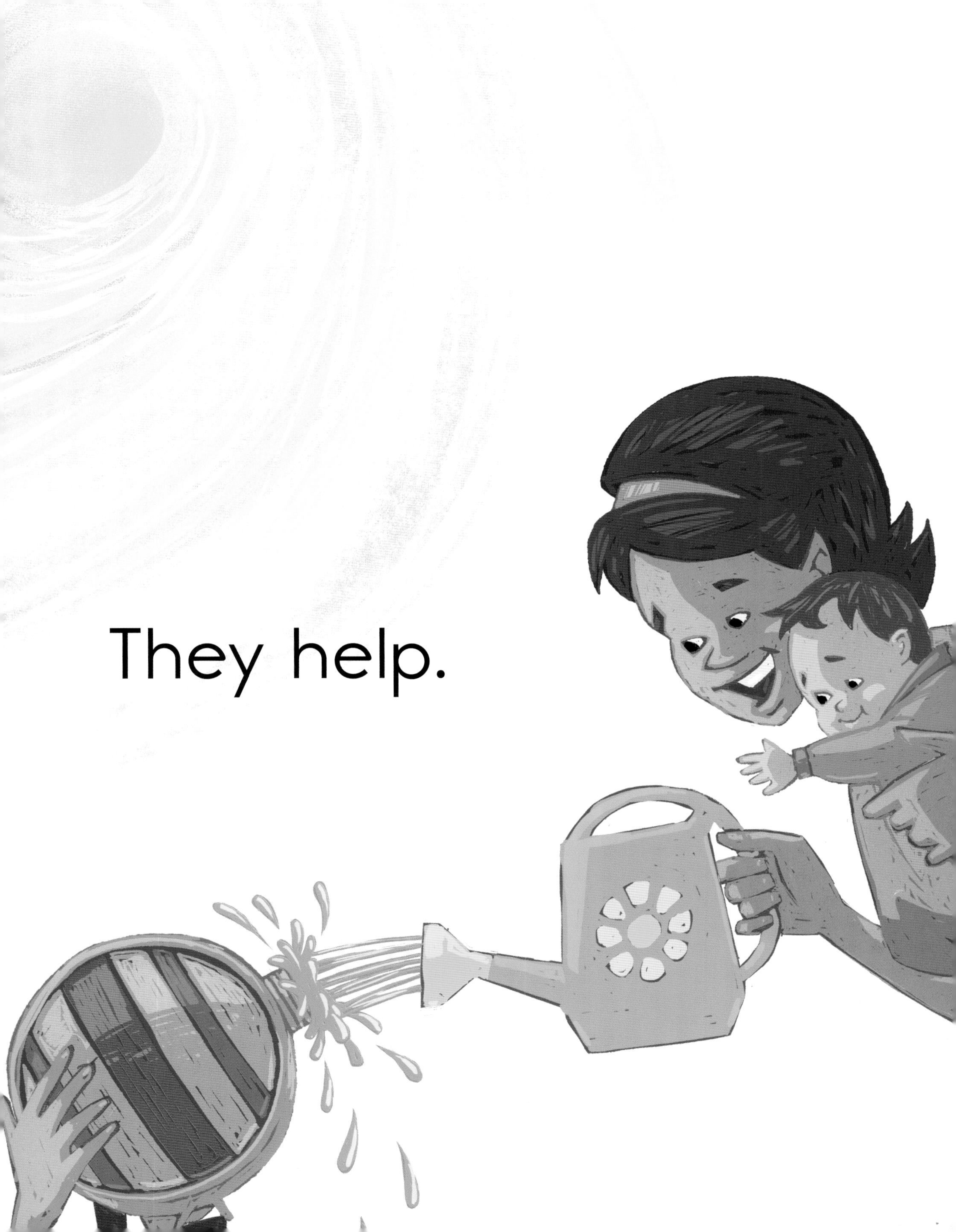

I go home.

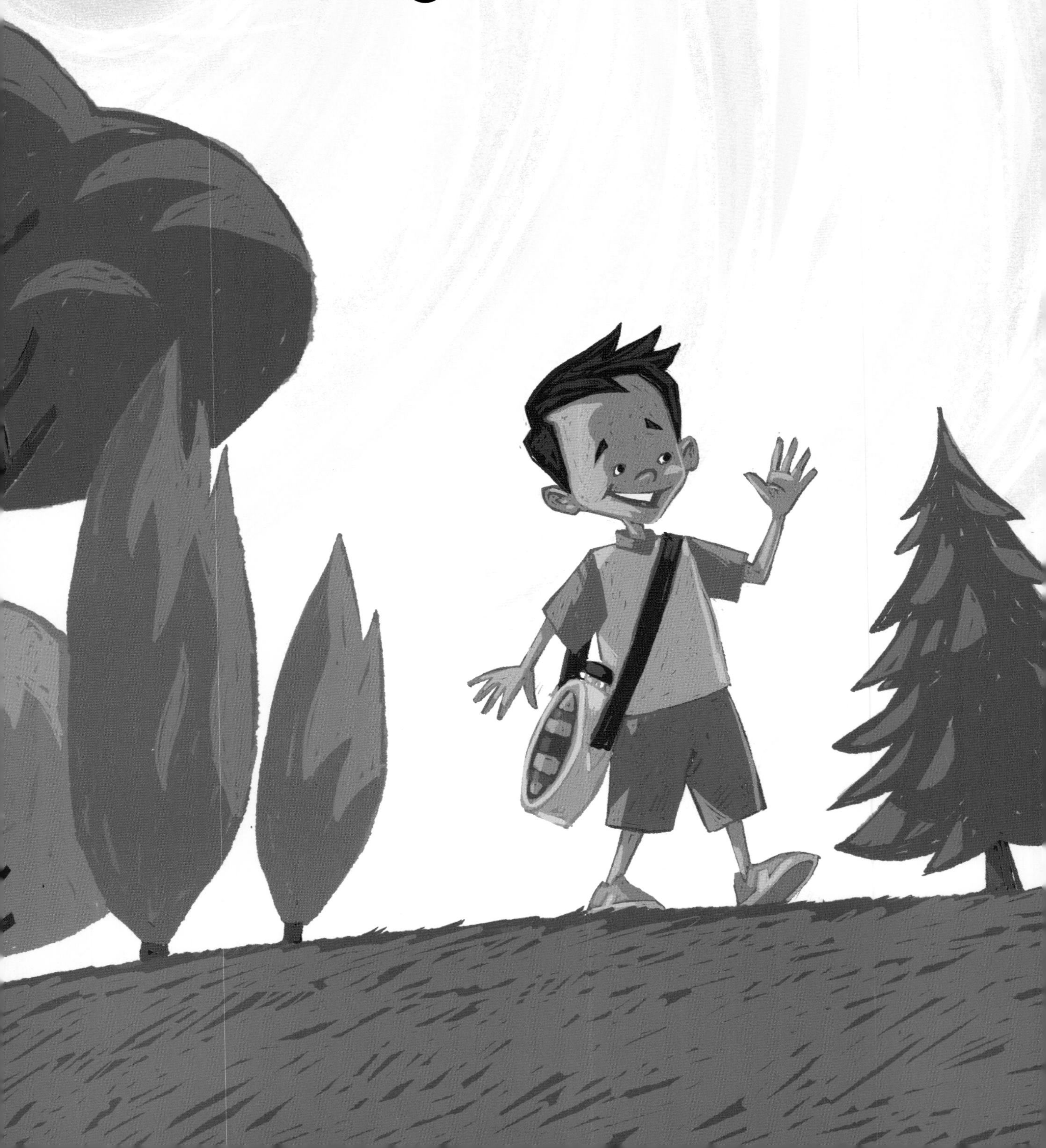

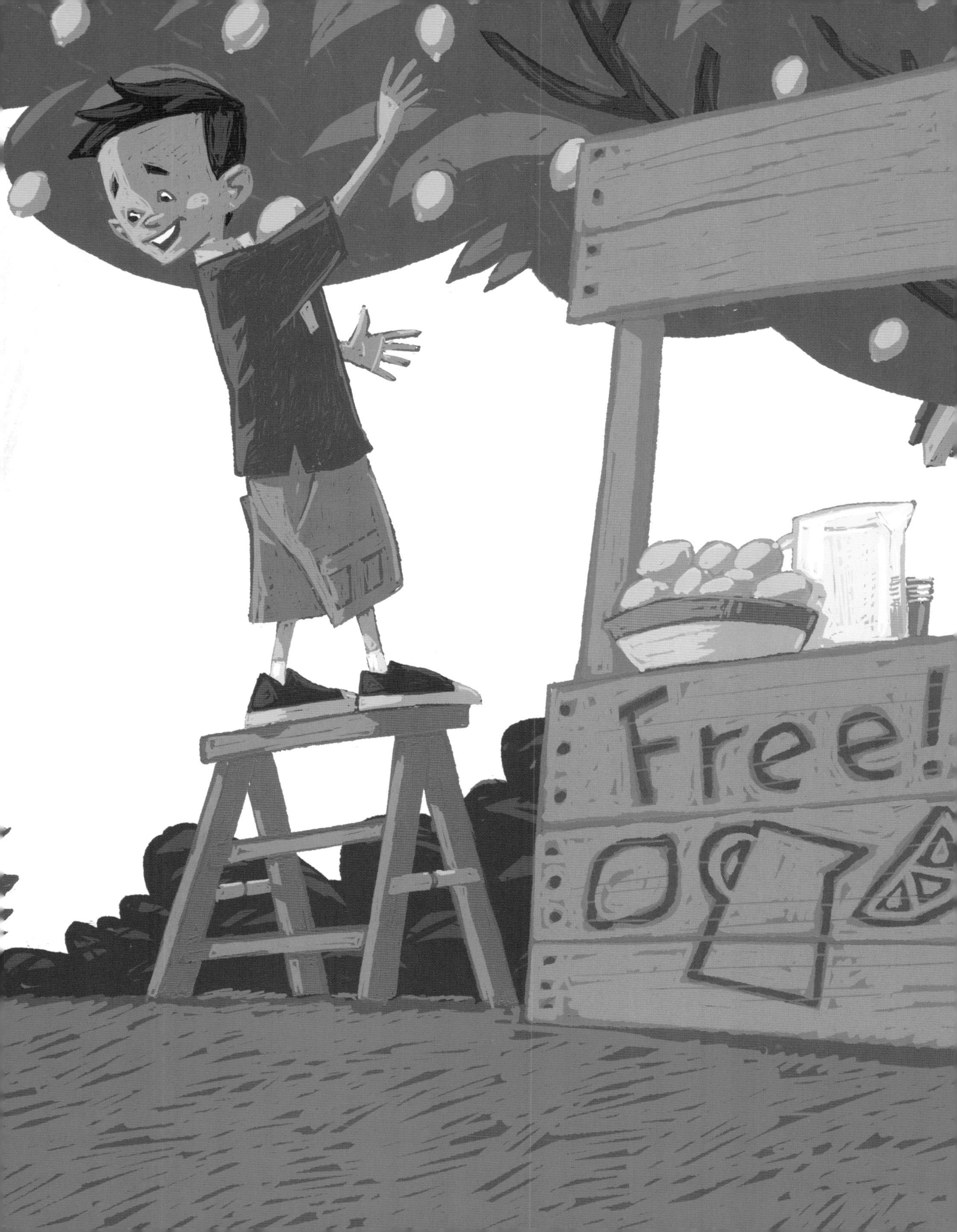
Free!

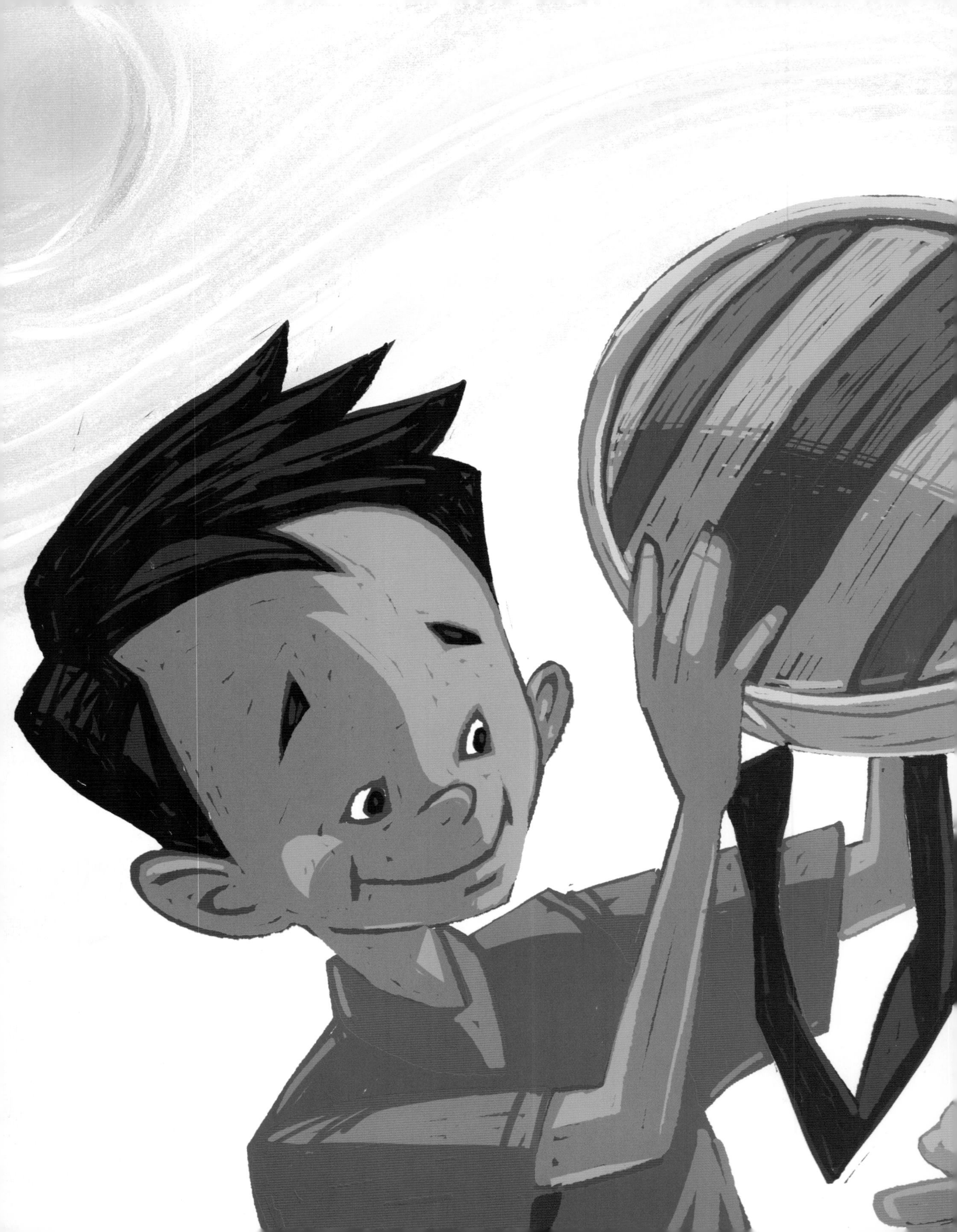

I help.

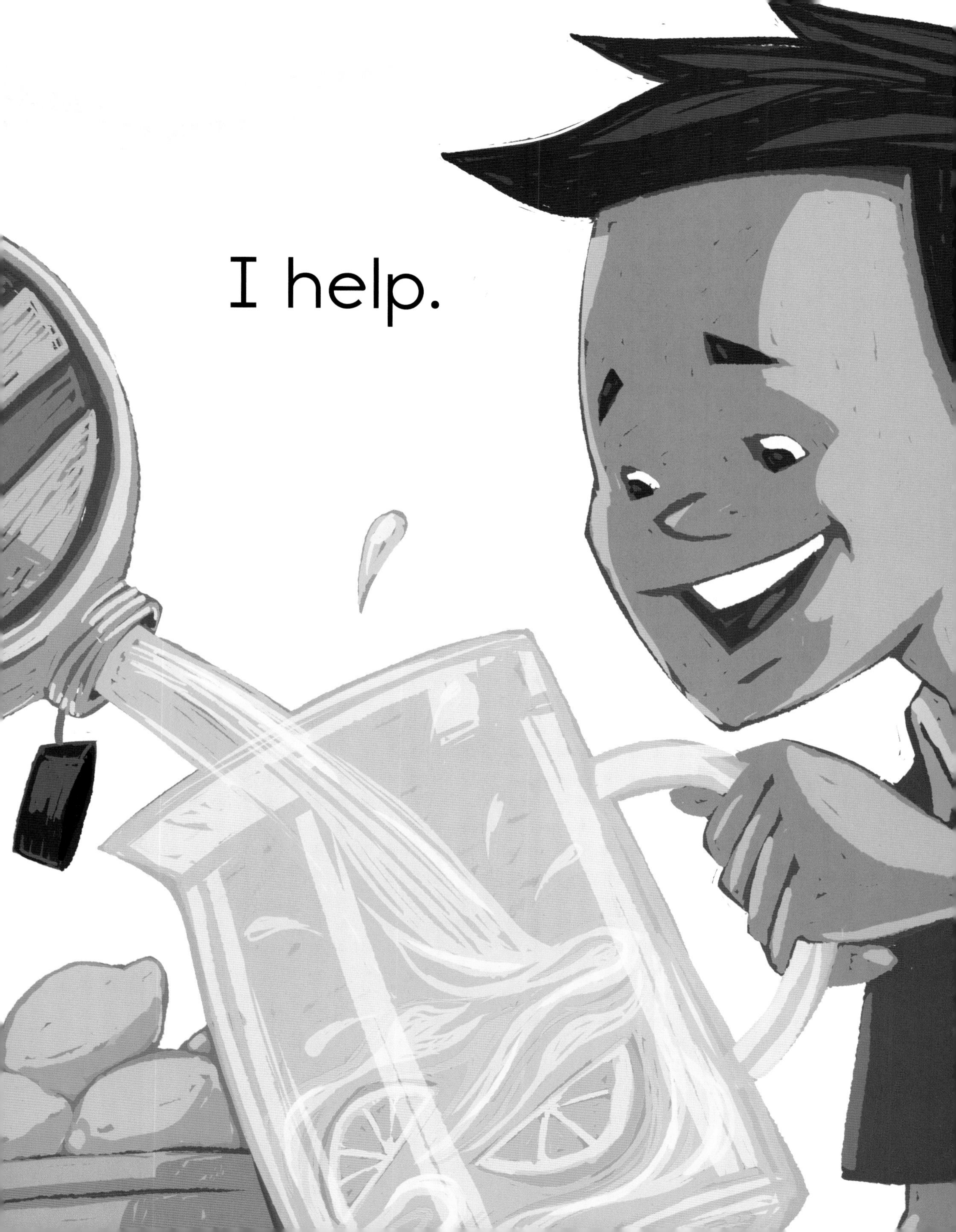

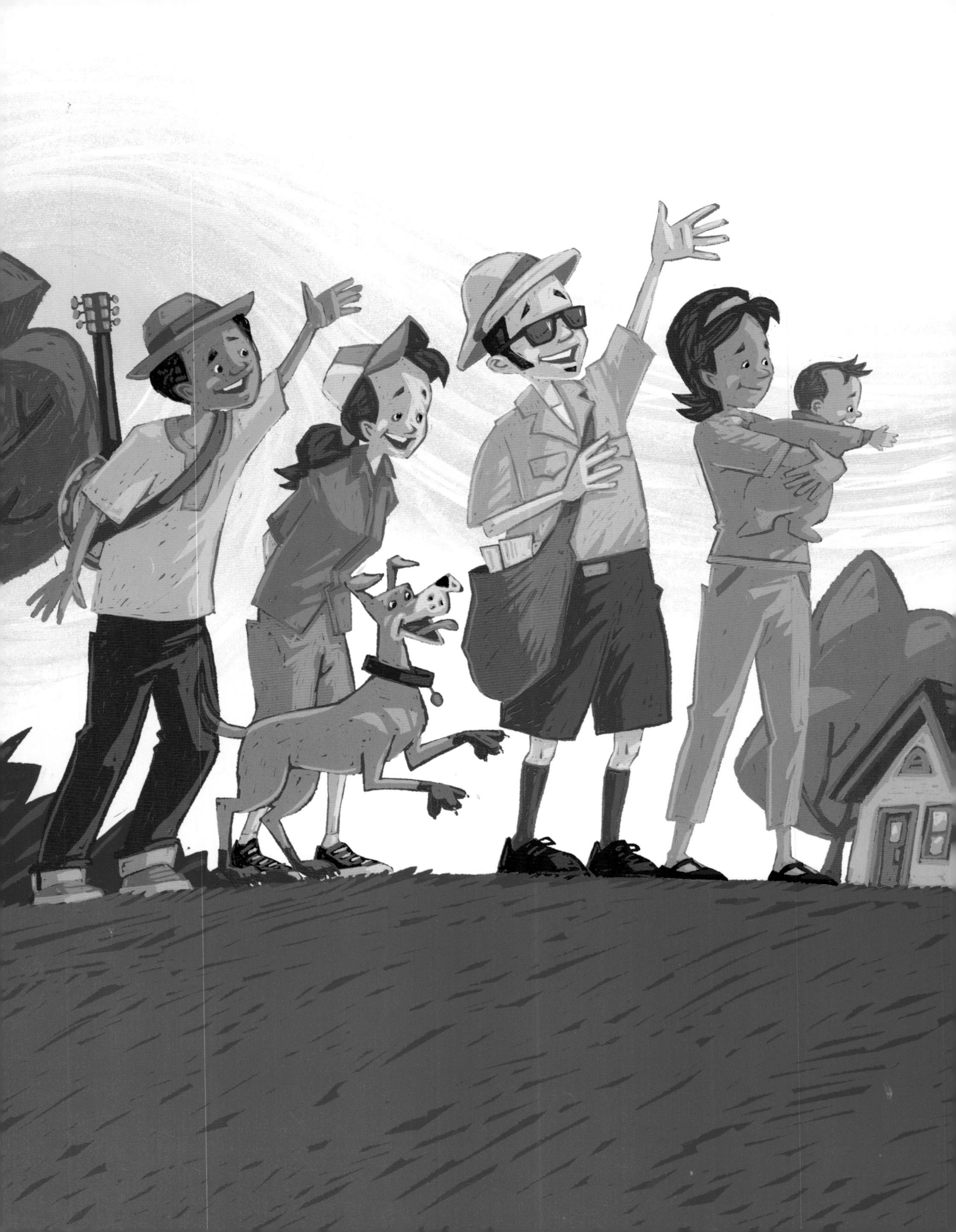

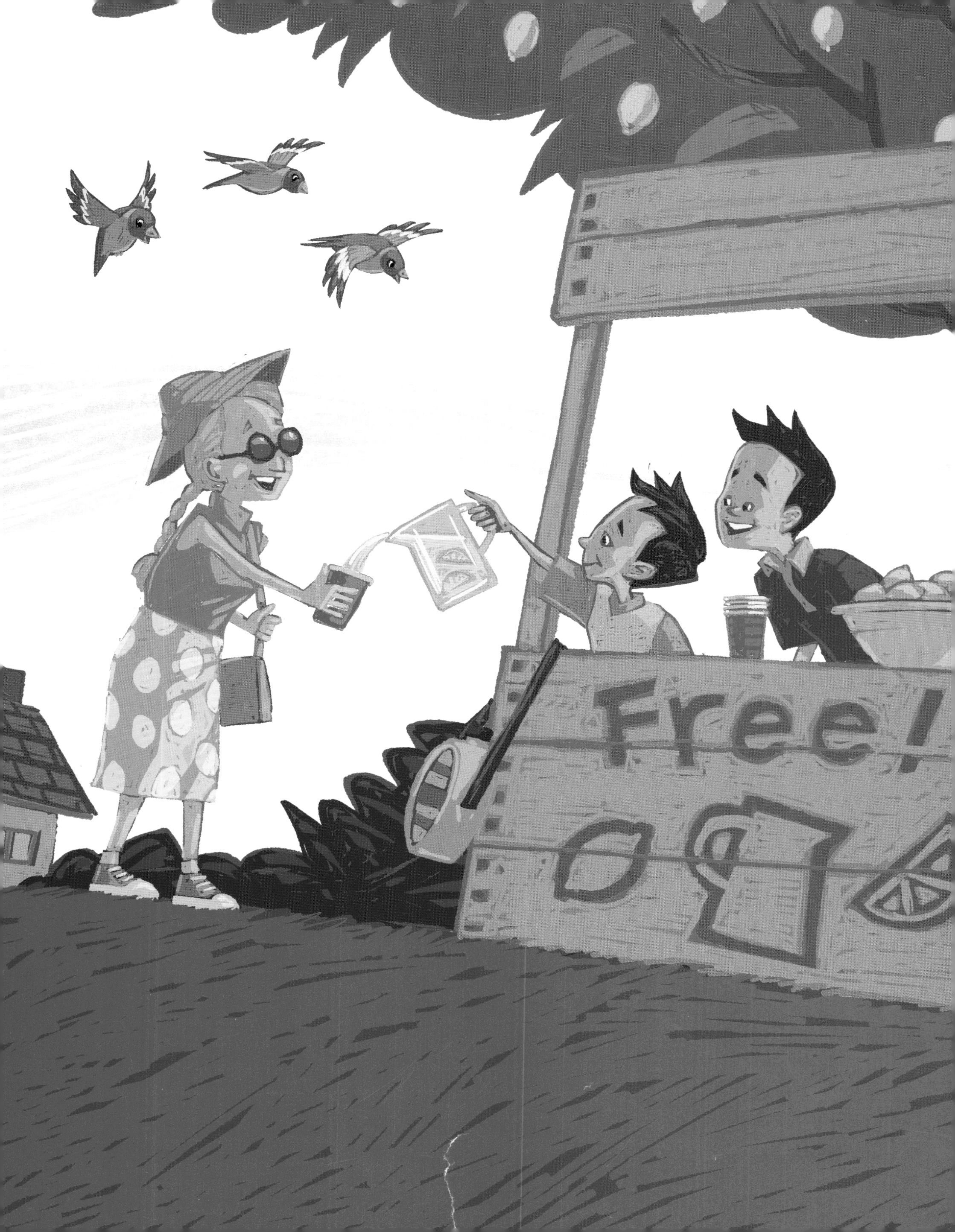
Free!

We help.

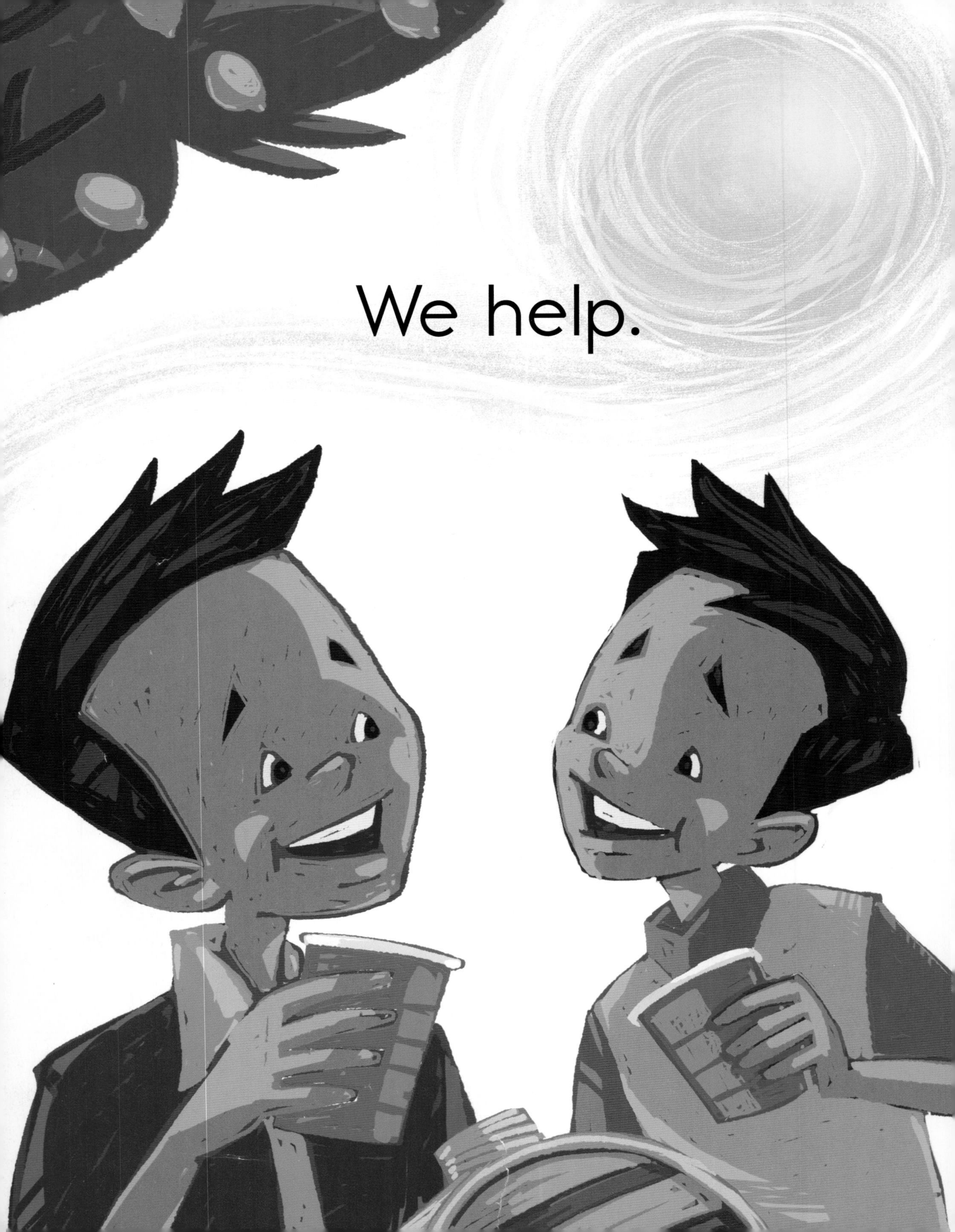